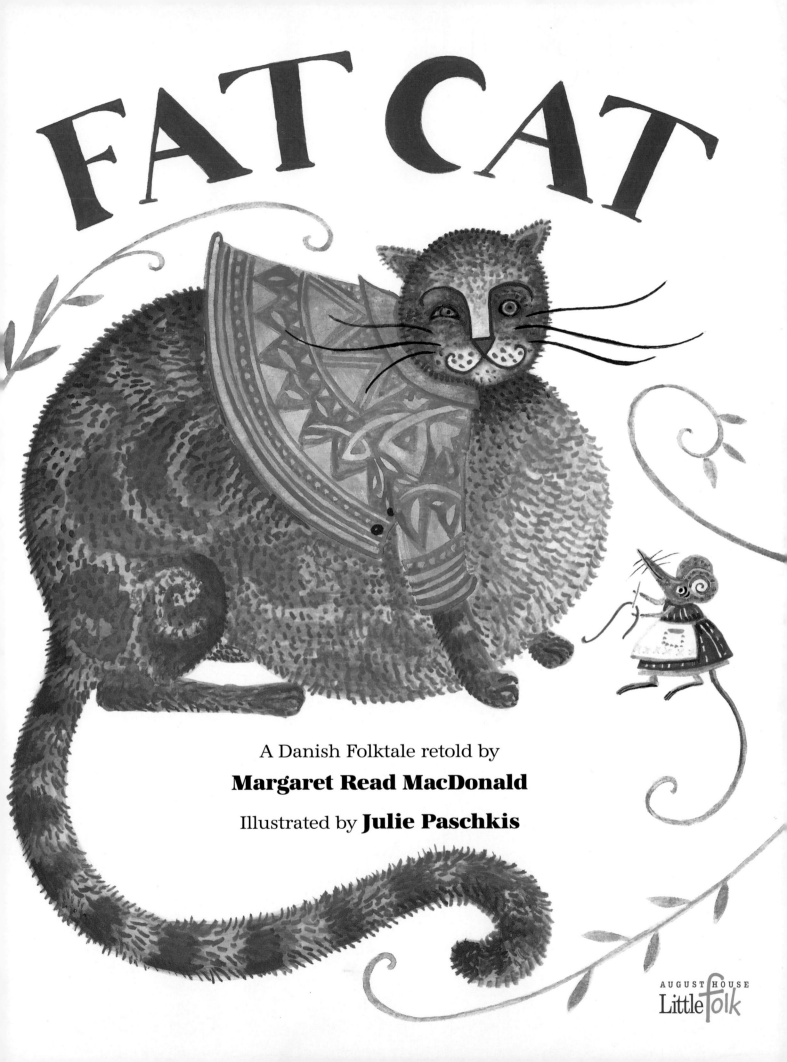

FAT CAT

A Danish Folktale retold by

Margaret Read MacDonald

Illustrated by **Julie Paschkis**

AUGUST HOUSE
LittleFolk

For Julie & Tom's Fat Cat —MRM

Text © 2001 by Margaret Read MacDonald
Illustrations © 2001 by Julie Paschkis.

Published 2001 by August House LittleFolk,
P.O. Box 3223, Little Rock, Arkansas 72203,
501-372-5450, www.augusthouse.com

Typography by Joy Freeman
Manufactured in Korea
10 9 8 7 6 5 4

LIBRARY OF CONGRESS CATALOGING-IN-PUBLICATION DATA
MacDonald, Margaret Read, 1940–
  Fat Cat : a Danish folktale / retold by Margaret Read MacDonald ;
illustrated by Julie Paschkis.
    p. cm.
  Summary: A greedy cat grows enormous as he eats everything
in sight, including his friends and neighbors who call him fat.
  ISBN 0-87483-616-6
  [1. Folklore—Denmark. 2. Cats—Folklore. 3. Mice—Folklore.]
  I. Paschkis, Julie, ill. II. Title.
PZ8.1.M15924 Fat 2001
398.2'09489'04529752—dc21
[E]   00-068939

For Adam—JP

A cat and a
mouse
kept house.

You can see
this was
not a good plan.

Cat was always
hungry.

Mouse was always
cooking.

One day Mouse baked 35 pies.

But … *SLIP, SLOP, SLUUURP!*
The greedy cat swallowed them all.

Mouse looked at Cat in alarm.

"MY, Cat! You sure are FAT!"

"I may be FAT,
   but I'm still a HUNGRY CAT!"

And out the door
clomped Cat,
meowing
greedily.

"Oh, I'm meow, meow FAT!
'Cause I'm a HUNGRY,
      HUNGRY,
         CAT!"

"I'm meow, meow FAT!
'Cause I'm a HUNGRY, HUNGRY CAT!"

A wash lady sudsing her clothes
looked up in surprise.

"My, CAT! You sure are FAT!"

"I may be FAT
But I'm still a
HUNGRY
CAT!"

And *SLIP SLOP SLUUURP!*
Cat swallowed the wash lady down.

Then *SLIP SLOP SLUUURP!*
Down went her soapsuds
and her laundry too!

"…BURP!"

"Oh, I'm meow,
meow
FAT!
'Cause I'm a
HUNGRY
HUNGRY
CAT!"

Up marched a company of soldiers
brandishing their swords.

"MY, Cat. You sure are FAT!"

"I may be FAT, but I'm still a HUNGRY CAT!"

And
SLIP SLOP SLUUURP!
Down
went
the soldiers.

Then
SLIP SLOP SLUURP!
Down
went
their swords, too!

"*…BURP!*"

"Oh, I'm meow, meow FAT!
'Cause I'm a HUNGRY, HUNGRY CAT!"

"I'm meow, meow FAT!
 'Cause I'm a
 HUNGRY, HUNGRY CAT!"

Along came the king
on his elephant.
The king and the elephant
stared in amazement.

"MY, Cat!
 You sure are FAT!"

"I may be FAT,
but I'm still a HUNGRY CAT!"

Then *SLIP SLOP SLUUURP!*
Down went the king.
And *SLIP SLOP SLUUURP!*
Down went his
elephant, too!

"...BURP!"

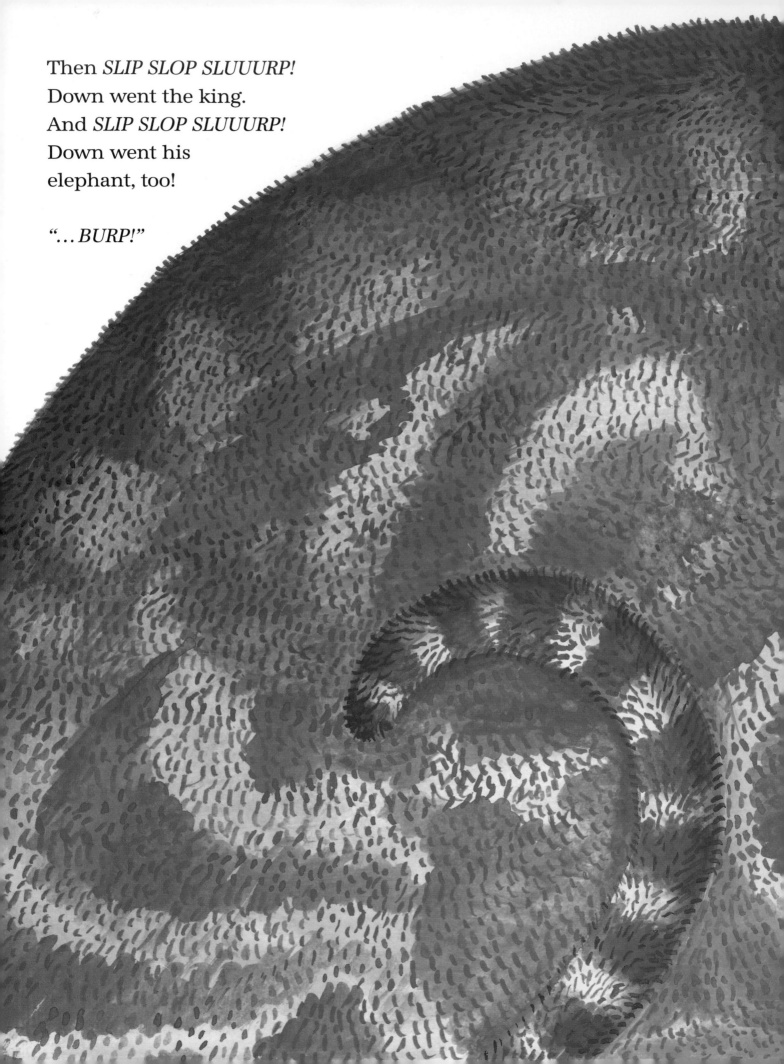

"I'm meow, meow FAT!
'Cause I'm a HUNGRY, HUNGRY CAT!"

Back home, Mouse was doing her mending.
She was sewing and snipping,
snipping and sewing,
when in clomped CAT!

"MY, Cat!
You sure got FAT!"

"I may be FAT, but I'm still a
HUNGRY CAT!"

And
SLIP
SLOP
SLUUURP!
Down went
Mouse!

Then
SLIP
SLOP
SLUUURP!
Down went
her scissors and
needle and thread too!

"…BURP!"

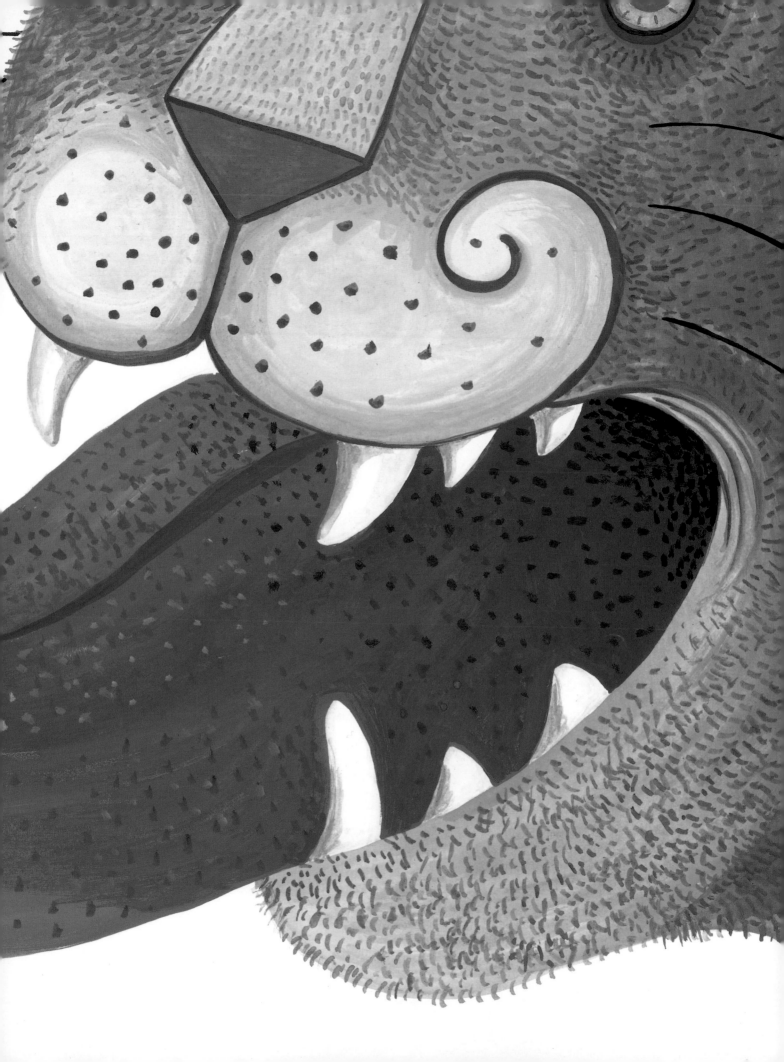

Mouse looked around Cat's huge stomach.
She saw the wash lady. She saw the soldiers.
She saw the king and his elephant too.
They were lying around looking miserable,
doing nothing at all.

"What is WRONG with you folks?" said Mouse.
"He may be a FAT cat.
 He may be a HUNGRY cat.
 But ENOUGH IS ENOUGH!"

Mouse took her little scissors
and poked a hole right
through that greedy cat's
stomach. She began to
snip

and

snip.

As soon as the hole was big enough,
out jumped the little mouse.

"Everybody OUT!" she cried.

Out stomped the wash lady,
dragging her washtub.
Out marched the soldiers,
waving their swords.
Out came the king,
leading his elephant.
And they all went about their business.

But Mouse spent the rest of the day
sewing up Cat's tummy.
After all, they were friends.

"Meow!
Meow!
MEOWWW!"

"Oh,
I'm
meow
meow
FLAT!
'Cause
I'm an
EMPTY
EMPTY
CAT!"

"I'm
meow
meow
FLAT!
'Cause
I'm an
EMPTY
EMPTY
CAT!"

After that,
Cat may have been hungry,
but he always left something
for Mouse.

And now, whenever
folks meet Cat
they are careful
to speak with respect.

"MY, Cat! You sure are fa-FANCY!"

"MY, Cat! You sure are fa-FABULOUS!"

"MY, Cat!
You sure are
fa-FANTASTIC!"

That's the meow, meow tale
of the FAT FAT CAT!

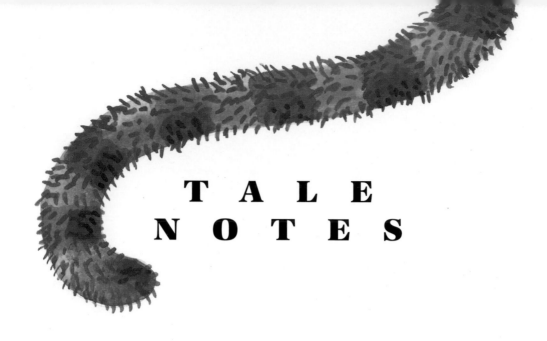

TALE NOTES

This story is a retelling of the folktale Motif Z33.2 The Fat Cat. Antti Aarne's *Types of the Folktale* lists many Swedish and Danish variants for Type 2027 The Fat Cat. An especially well-known version is that appearing in the Norwegian folktale collections of Peter Asbjørnsen and Jørgen Moe. The notion of a greedy animal consuming everyone it meets is popular worldwide. For other variants, see motifs Z33.2-Z33.7 in *The Storyteller's Sourcebook* by Margaret Read MacDonald (Detroit: Gale Research, 1982). You will find references there to the tale from India of the cat and the parrot, the Russian story of the clay pot boy, the American tale of the greedy bear, and others.

My telling of "The Fat Cat" was strongly influenced by another tale I have told for years, "Kuratko the Terrible" (in *The Shoemaker's Apron: A Second Book of Czechoslovak Fairy Tales and Folktales* by Parker Fillmore [New York: Harcourt Brace, 1919]). In that tale the greedy rooster Kuratko eats everyone in sight and Kotsor the cat cuts them out.

—MRM